Meri's Dream

by Jan Albach Jewell

with illustrations by

Jan Albach Jewell • J.M. Steinmetz • Jonathan Thomson

11220 120th Ave. NE, Kirkland, WA 98033
Tel: 425-250-1003 * 800-424-7843 (orders only) * Fax: 425-641-2028
JanJ@BirthdayExpress.com * www.BirthdayExpress.com

Library of Congress Control Number: 2001117187
Library of Congress Cataloging-in-Publication Data

Jewell, Jan, 1957 -
Meri's Dream written by Jan Albach Jewell; illustrated by J. M. Steinmetz,
Jonathan Thomson and Jan A. Jewell.
p. cm.
Summary: A little Unicorn discovers the joy one receives when helping others.

ISBN 0-9710083-0-2 (hardcover)
1. Unicorns--Fiction. 2. Forests--Fiction. 3. Owl--Fiction. 4. Helping others--Fiction.
I. Jan A. Jewell, J. M. Steinmetz & Jonathan Thomson
II. Illustrations. III. Title.

Published in the United States of America
Printed by Wing King Tong Co. Ltd., Hong Kong

Book Designer:
Jan Albach Jewell, Birthday Express, Kirkland, WA

Dedicated with love to my family —
Mike, David, Maia, Sebastian and Sapphire —
who have made my life so rich.

Jan Albach Jewell

❤

Once there was a little unicorn named Meri. She lived with her mother inside a giant, hollowed-out tree in a vast forest, and slept in a cozy nest made of star-shaped leaves. One morning Meri awoke with her heart pounding in her chest. She had dreamt that her mother was lost in the deepest part of the forest. Quickly, she scrambled to her feet and looked outside, but she couldn't see her mother anywhere!

Soon her mother returned from gathering berries for breakfast, and Meri, still trembling from fear, described her frightening dream. "Don't worry my precious little one, it was just a dream," her mother said with a loving nuzzle. "I'll always be here for you." Relieved, Meri soon forgot about her dream and together they bounded off into the lush meadow that bordered the forest. It was a beautiful day, but Meri found herself shivering in the cool autumn breeze. As she turned her face upward to feel the warmth of the sun, she noticed all the apples growing in the trees. She remembered the beautiful, sweet-smelling white flowers that had appeared in the same trees that spring, and how they had quickly grown into baby apples. She had been waiting impatiently all summer for them to turn into shiny red apples so they would be ready to eat!

Meri was so excited that she began to leap wildly into the air, attempting to reach the luscious red apples; but she was too small to reach even the lowest limb. Her mother reached up and used her sleek golden horn to gently nudge an apple from the tree. To Meri's surprise, juice splattered her in the eye when when the apple fell, right on her little horn and was speared by it! With a slight chuckle, her mother removed the apple and cleaned the juice from her daughter's face, thinking to herself, "I couldn't do that again, no matter how hard I tried!" "Thanks mother!" Meri said as she nibbled the tasty fruit. "I wish I could do things to help you," she said. Her mother thought for a moment and then replied, "You'll feel good about yourself when you help someone else, and your heart will sing all day!"

Meri spent the rest of the day playing in the meadow and the neighboring woods. There she came upon a snowy white owl who was flapping his wings in a panic and creating quite a ruckus. As she got closer, she was surprised to see that he was caught in a thicket of sharp, painful thorns! Using her horn to pry the thorns apart, Meri freed the owl, who quickly flew up into the air saying, "Thank-hoo, Thank-hoo. I thought I'd never get out of there!" Meri thought to herself, "Now I've helped someone. This must be what my mother was talking about." The owl then asked, "How can I repay you for your kindness?" Meri thought about what her mother had just taught her and replied, "You feel good about yourself when you help someone else, and your heart will sing all day!"

Meri and her new friend played together for the rest of the afternoon. When she realized that darkness had quietly descended upon the forest, and that clouds laden with snow were beginning to form in the distance, she knew it was time to go home. Meri said goodbye to her feathered friend and headed for the safety of home. She wanted to get back before it got too dark, so she began running as fast as she could. Soon she found herself panting and gasping for breath, so much that her sides began to ache. By the time she returned home to the warmth of the hollow tree, it was bitterly cold outside and it had begun to snow.

With her teeth chattering, and feeling tired after playing all day long, Meri plopped herself down in the snug nest that lay inside the hollow tree. She couldn't see her mother but figured that she must be nearby. She tried to stay awake, but her eyelids grew heavier and heavier, and it wasn't long before she dozed off to sleep. While she slept, giant snowflakes settled into deep snow drifts, and the only sound to break through the silence of the forest was the howling wind as it swept through the darkened meadow.

While her daughter slept peacefully in the comfort of their hollow tree, Meri's mother was struck by how a forest that had always seemed so welcoming was now unfamiliar in the midst of the blinding snowstorm. Her cries for help went unanswered and were lost in the enormous, bigness of the empty forest. Her heart began to race as she realized that she was unable to find her way home.

Suddenly and with a swiftness Meri's mother had never witnessed
before, a snowy white owl swooped down through the trees and cut into the silence of
the shadowy night. "What are hoo doing out in this snowstorm?" he asked. Frightened
by the appearance of the owl, Meri's mother jumped back and replied in a shaky voice,
"I seem to have gotten lost! Can you help me find my way out of the forest?" "I can try,"
replied the owl. He spread his enormous wings and flew high into the sky to look for
the open meadow where all the unicorns lived. With his keen vision and
bird's-eye view from above the trees, he safely guided
the shivering unicorn out of the forest.

After what seemed like hours of trudging through ever-deepening snow drifts, Meri's mother finally recognized familiar surroundings and mustered enough strength to whisper gratefully, "I can find my way home from here. Thank you owl. How can I ever repay you for your kindness?"

The owl remembered how Meri had helped him when
he was caught in the thicket of thorns. He puffed out his chest
and replied, "You'll feel good about yourself when you help someone
else, and your heart will sing all day!" Meri's mother looked at the owl
in surprise, remembering how she had recently told Meri exactly the same thing!

Meanwhile, Meri awoke from her nap amidst the
tranquility of the snow-blanketed forest only to realize that her mother
was not there. The only sound she could hear was her heart pounding
as she thought of how the terrifying dream of her mother
becoming lost in the forest had come true.

Restless and now trembling with fear, Meri rushed
outside and began searching the area around the hollow tree to look for
her mother. At that same moment, relieved to be home, her mother came around the
other side of the tree, but was heartbroken to see that the nest made of
star-shaped leaves was empty.

Overcome with fear that Meri had also
become lost in the snowstorm, her heart leaped with
joy when she glimpsed a flicker of Meri's tail as it disappeared
around the opposite side of the hollow tree. She rushed to Meri's
side, and as her eyes filled with tears of happiness, gave thanks
to be home safe again with her beautiful daughter.

About the Author

Photo by Christine Born

Jan Jewell

Jan Jewell was born and raised in Dallas, Texas. Early in her career, Ms. Jewell worked as an apprentice to a goldsmith in Copenhagen, Denmark, and honed her skills as an independent jewelry designer in Houston; Salem, New Hampshire; Boston; and the San Francisco Bay area, quickly securing a loyal international clientele. In 1987 Jan opened a jewelry salon in Palo Alto, California, where she designed and manufactured high-end jewelry for five years before moving to the Pacific Northwest.

After nearly losing her third child when he was born 3 months premature in 1992, Jan and her husband Mike decided to redirect their efforts and founded Birthday Express, a catalog company with a mission to help busy parents celebrate the lives of their children. Today she lives in the Seattle, Washington area with her husband Mike, and has four children, David, Maia, Sebastian and Sapphire.

About the Illustrators

J. M. Steinmetz

J. Max Steinmetz was born in Leominster, Wales, and later moved with his family to Boston, Massachusetts. He has contributed to numerous comic strips and books. The playful imagery of the apple falling on Meri's horn is his favorite illustration in Meri's Dream. He currently resides in Seattle, Washington, with his cat Rufus, whom he adopted from PAWS.

Jonathan Thomson

Jonathan Thomson was born in New Jersey and has worked as a sculptor and designer for such well-known companies as Walt Disney, Warner Bros., Lenox and Glass Eye Studios. Jonathan is currently employed by Birthday Express as a sculptor and illustrator. He enjoyed working on Meri's Dream because it allowed him to conceptualize and shape the story by means of illustration. He lives outside of Seattle, Washington, with his wife Kari and their two daughters, Alyssa and Ashley.